TITCHY WITCH

AND THE MAGIC PARTY

ROSE IMPEY ★ KATHARINE McEWEN

ORCHARD

Titchy-witch

Victor

Eric

Wendel

Weeny-witch

Witchy-witch

Cat-a-bogus

It was almost Halloween.
Witchy-witch and Wendel were
having a big party.

Titchy-witch wanted a party too.
"Of course, my little bewitcher,"
said Mum. "Cat-a-bogus will
do the food."

Oh, really?

Titchy-witch wanted all
her favourite things.

Mounds of maggot and
marmalade sandwiches,
piles of slug and pickle pizzas,
mountains of frogspawn jelly
and a colossal cake.

Yum! Yum!

Is that all?

9

Titchy-witch made a list of party games too.

1. Musical broomsticks.

2. Pass the cauldron.

3. Crab-apple bobbing.

4.

And prizes!
"Big bags of Wiggly Wagglies and
Drobble-drops and Squibblies."

"I hope no-one's sick," said
Cat-a-bogus.

But then Titchy-witch didn't know
who to invite to her party.

Primrose was really prissy.

And Gobby-goblin poked her all the time.

And Wilfy-wolf played
tricks on her.

And Clever Jack was the
teacher's pet.

"Haven't got any friends," said
Titchy-witch.
"Well, a party's a good way to
make some," said Wendel.

But when the party arrived,
Titchy-witch didn't think
she was going to enjoy
it very much.

She scowled when Clever
Jack won all the Drobble-drops.

She gritted her fangs when
Gobby-goblin cheated at
Crab-Apple Bobbing.

And when Primrose won at
Musical Broomsticks, she was so
cross she wiggled her nose...

...and made Primrose's broomstick disappear.

Mum and Dad told her to hand
round the food and be
a good little witch.
But she wasn't.

Suddenly Primrose
had a tail.

Clever Jack grew a pair of
rabbit's ears.

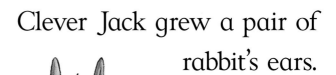

Gobby-goblin started
breathing fire.

And Wilfy-Wolf found he could fly.

Mum and Dad nearly put a stop to it.

But everyone was having such a good time.

"You are clever," said Clever Jack.
"I wish I was a witch, like you,"
said Primrose.

Even Gobby-goblin asked Titchy-witch to come to his cave for tea.

At the end of the party Cat-a-bogus was waiting at the door. He made sure everyone went home the same as they had come.

Well, almost every one.

"Please let me keep it," begged Primrose. "Just till Monday." "All right," said Titchy-witch.

Primrose gave her a big hug.
"You're my best friend ever,"
she said.

TITCHY WITCH

BY ROSE IMPEY   ILLUSTRATED BY KATHARINE McEWEN

Enjoy a little more magic with all the Titchy-witch tales:

Orchard Books are available from all good
bookshops, or can be ordered from our website:
www.orchardbooks.co.uk
or telephone 01235 827702, or fax 01235 827703.

Prices and availability are subject to change.